The Best Of BOB DYLAN

volume 2

Exclusive distributors:
Music Sales Limited, 8/9 Frith Street, London W1D 3JB, England.
Music Sales Pty Limited, 120 Rothschild Avenue, Rosebery, NSW 2018, Australia.

Order No.AM967186 ISBN: 0-7119-8476-X
This book © Copyright 2000 by Wise Publications.

Music arranged by Derek Jones.
Music engraved by Paul Ewers Music Design.
Cover Image courtesy of Sony Records.

Printed in the United Kingdom by Printwise (Haverhill) Limited, Suffolk.

Your Guarantee of Quality:
As publishers, we strive to produce every book to the highest commercial standards.
The music has been freshly engraved and, whilst endeavouring to retain the original
running order of the recorded album, the book has been carefully designed to minimise
awkward page turns and to make playing from it a real pleasure.
Particular care has been given to specifying acid-free, neutral-sized paper
made from pulps which have not been elemental chlorine bleached.
This pulp is from farmed sustainable forests and was produced with special regard for the environment.
Throughout, the printing and binding have been planned to ensure a sturdy,
attractive publication which should give years of enjoyment.
If your copy fails to meet our high standards, please inform us and we will gladly replace it.

Music Sales' complete catalogue describes thousands of titles and
is available in full colour sections by subject, direct from Music Sales Limited.
Please state your areas of interest and send a cheque/postal order for £1.50 for postage to:
Music Sales Limited, Newmarket Road, Bury St. Edmunds, Suffolk IP33 3YB.

www.musicsales.com

Wise Publications
London/New York/Sydney/Paris/Copenhagen/Madrid/Tokyo

THINGS HAVE CHANGED

Words & Music by Bob Dylan

wo-man on my lap— and she's drink-ing cham - pagne.—

Got white skin, got as - sas-sin's eyes,—

I'm look-ing up in-to the sapph-ire— tin-ted skies,- I'm well— dressed, wait-

- ing on the last———— train.—

Stand-ing on the gal-lows with my head in the noose.

A-ny mi-nute now I'm ex-pect-ing all hell to break

loose. Peo-ple are cra-zy and times

are strange, I'm locked in tight, I'm out-ta range. I

used to care_____ but_____ things have_____ changed._____

Guitar

1-3.

Verse 2:

This place ain't doing me any good
I'm in the wrong town, I should be in Hollywood
Just for a second there I thought I saw something move
Gonna take dancing lessons do the jitterbug rag
Ain't no shortcuts, gonna dress in drag
Only a fool in here would think he's got anything to prove.

Lot of water under the bridge, lot of other stuff too
Don't get up gentlemen, I'm only passing through.

People are crazy *etc.*

Verse 3:

I've been walking forty miles of bad road
If the bible is right, the world will explode
I've been trying to get as far away from myself as I can
Some things are too hot to touch
The human mind can only stand so much
You can't win with a losing hand.

Feel like falling in love with the first woman I meet
Putting her in a wheel barrow and wheeling her down the street.

People are crazy *etc.*

Verse 4:

I hurt easy, I just don't show it
You can hurt someone and not even know it
The next sixty seconds could be like an eternity
Gonna get low down, gonna fly high
All the truth in the world adds up to one big lie
I'm in love with a woman who don't even appeal to me

Mr Jinx and Miss Lucy, they jumped in the lake
I'm not that eager to make a mistake.

People are crazy *etc.*

A HARD RAIN'S A-GONNA FALL

Words & Music by Bob Dylan

stum-bled on the side - of twelve mis-ty moun-tains, I've

walked and I've crawled- on six crook-ed high-ways, I've

stepped in the mid-dle of sev-en sad for-ests, I've

been out in front of a do-zen dead o-ceans, I've been

what did you see my darl-in' young one?   I saw a

new-born ba - by with wild wolves all a - round it,   I saw a

high-way of dia-monds with no-bo-dy on — it,   I

saw a black branch with blood that kept drip-pin',—   I saw a

room full of men__ with their ham-mers a - bleed - in',__ I

saw a white lad-der all cov-ered with wa - ter, I saw

ten thou-sand talk-ers whose tongues were all bro - ken,__ I saw

guns and sharp swords in the hands__ of young chil - dren,__ and it's a

hard, it's a hard, it's a hard, and it's a hard, it's a

hard rain's _____ a - gon - na fall. _____

1.

3. And

2.

4. Oh

what did you meet my blue - eyed _____ son? And

met a young girl, she gave— me a rain-bow,— I

met one man who was wound-ed in love,— I

met a-noth-er man— who was wound-ed in hat-red,— and it's a

hard, it's a hard, it's a hard, it's a hard, it's a

hard rain's_____ a - gon-na fall._____

5. And

what-'ll you do now my blue-eyed___ son? And

what-'ll you do now___ my darl-in' young one? I'm a -

17

tell it and speak it and think it and breath it, and re - flect

from the moun - tain so all souls can see it, and I'll

stand on the o - cean un - til I start sink - ing, and I'll know

my song well be - fore I start sing - ing, and it's a

Verse 3:
And what did you hear, my blue-eyed son?
And what did you hear, my darling young one?
I heard the sound of a thunder, that roared out a warnin'
I heard the roar of a wave that could drown the whole world
I heard one hundred drummers whose hands where a-blazin'
I heard ten thousand whisperin' and nobody listenin'
I heard one person starve, I heard many people laughin'
I heard the song of a poet who died in the gutter
I heard the sound of a clown who cried in the alley.

And it's a hard *etc.*

IT AIN'T ME BABE

Words & Music by Bob Dylan

to o - pen each and ev - 'ry door, _____ but it ain't

me, ___ babe, no, __ no, no it ain't me, babe, it ain't

me you're look - in' for, babe.

Harmonica

2. Go light - ly from the ledge, babe, go __

Verse 3:
Go melt back into the night, babe
Everything inside is made of stone
There's nothing in here moving
An' anyway I'm not alone.

You say you're looking for someone
Who'll pick you up each time you fall
To gather flowers constantly
An' to come each time you call
A lover for your life an' nothing more.

But it ain't me *etc.*

POSITIVELY 4TH STREET

Words & Music by Bob Dylan

you just stood there grin - ning.— You got a—

lot - ta nerve— to say you got - ta help - ing— hand to lend,

you just want— to be on the side— that's win - ning.

2. You say I let you down, you know it's not like that,—
(Verses 3-6 see block lyrics)

if you're so hurt why___ then don't___ you

show it?   You say you lost your faith,_ but

that's not where_ it's at,_____ you had no faith to lose_

and you know it.___

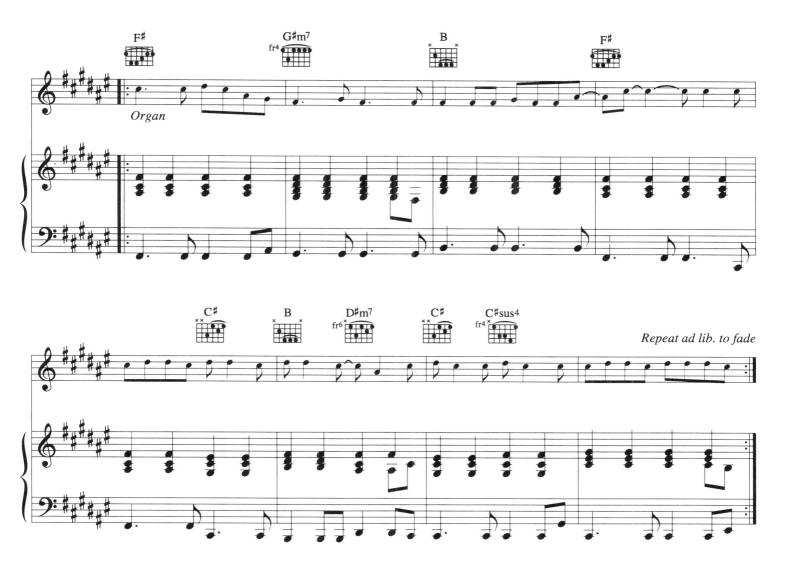

Verse 3:
I know the reason
That you talk behind my back
I used to be among the crowd
You're in with.

Do you take me for such a fool
To think I'd make contact
With the one who tries to hide
What he don't know to begin with?

Verse 4:
You see me on the street
You always act surprised
You say, "How are you?" "Good luck"
But you don't mean it.

When you know as well as me
You'd rather see me paralyzed
Why don't you just come out once
And scream it.

Verse 5:
No, I do not feel that good
When I see the heartbreaks you embrace
If I was a master thief
Perhaps I'd rob them.

And now I know you're dissatisfied
With your position and your place
Don't you understand
It's not my problem.

Verse 6:
I wish that for just one time
You could stand inside my shoes
And just for that one moment
I could be you.

Yes, I wish that for just one time
You could stand inside my shoes
You'd know what a drag it is
To see you.

SUBTERRANEAN HOMESICK BLUES

Words & Music by Bob Dylan

Moderate blues rock

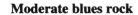

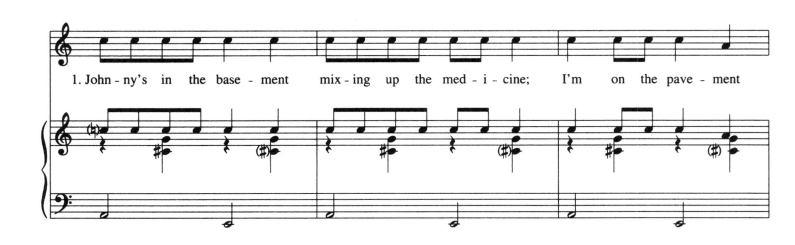

1. John-ny's in the base-ment mix-ing up the med-i-cine; I'm on the pave-ment

think-ing a-bout the gov-ern-ment. The man in the trench coat,

badge out, laid off, says he's got a bad cough; wants to get it paid off.

Look out, kid, __ it's some-thin' you did; __ God knows when __ but you're

do - in' it a - gain! You bet - ter duck down the al - ley - way

look - in' for a new friend; the man in the coon - skin cap by the big pen

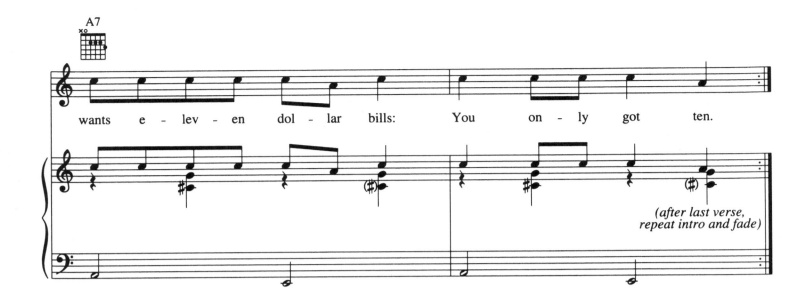

A7

wants e – lev – en dol – lar bills: You on – ly got ten.

(after last verse, repeat intro and fade)

2. Maggie comes fleet foot
    Face full of black soot
    Talkin' at the heat put
    Plants in the bed but
    The phone's tapped any-way
    Maggie says that many say
    They must bust in early May
    Orders from the D.A.
    Look out kid
    Don't matter what you did
    Walk on your tip toes
    Don't try "No Doz"
    Better stay away from those
    That carry around a fire hose
    Keep a clean nose
    Watch the plain clothes
    You don't need a weather man
    To know which way the wind blows.

3. Get sick, get well
    Hang around a ink well
    Ring bell, hard to tell
    If anything is goin' to sell
    Try hard, get barred
    Get back, write braille
    Get jailed, jump bail
    Join the army, if you fail
    Look out kid, you're gonna get hit
    But users, cheaters
    Six time losers
    Hang around the theatres
    Girl by the whirlpool
    Lookin' for a new fool
    Don't follow leaders
    Watch the parkin' meters

4. Ah get born, keep warm
    Short pants, romance, learn to dance
    Get dressed, get blessed
    Try to be a success
    Please her, please him, buy gifts
    Don't steal, don't lift
    Twenty years of schoolin'
    And they put you on the day shift
    Look out kid they keep it all hid
    Better jump down a manhole
    Light yourself a candle, don't wear sandals
    Try to avoid the scandals
    Don't wanna be a bum
    You better chew gum
    The pump don't work
    'Cause the vandals took the handles.

HIGHWAY 61 REVISITED

Words & Music by Bob Dylan

say,— "No."— Abe— say,— "What?"— God— say,— "You can do what you want Abe, but— the next time you see me com-in'— you— bet-ter run."

Well Abe— says, "Where you want this kill-in' done?"— God—

says, "Out on High - way six - ty one."

1-3.

2. Well

4.

5. Now the

ro - vin' gam - bler he was ve - ry bored,— tryin' to cre - ate a next

world war.— He found a pro-mo-ter who near-ly fell off the floor, he said

I nev-er en-gaged in this kind of thing be - fore,— but yes— I think it can be

ve - ry ea - si - ly done.

We'll just put— some bleach - ers out

in the sun___ and have it on___ High - way six - ty one.___

Repeat ad lib. to fade

Verse 2:
Well Georgia Sam he had a bloody nose
Welfare Department they wouldn't give him no clothes
He asked poor Howard where can I go
Howard said there's only one place I know
Sam said tell me quick man I got to run
Ol' Howard just pointed with his gun
And said that way down on Highway 61.

Verse 3:
Well Mack the Finger said to Louie the King
I got forty red, white and blue shoe strings
And a thousand telephones that don't ring
Do you know where I can get rid of these things?
And Louie the King said let me think for a minute son
And he said yes I think it can be easily done
Just take everything down to Highway 61.

Verse 4:
Now the fifth daughter on the twelfth night
Told the first father that things weren't right
My complexion she said is much too white
He said come here and step into the light he says hmm you're right
Let me tell the second mother this has been done
But the second mother was with the seventh son
And they were both out on Highway 61.

I WANT YOU

Words & Music by Bob Dylan

Interlude:

all my fa - thers, they've gone down,_ True love they've_ been with-

out it. But all their daugh - ters put me down 'Cause I don't think a - bout_

_ it.

D.S.al Fine
(3rd and 4th Verses)

3. Well, I re -

Additional Lyrics

3. Well, I return to the Queen of Spades
   And talk with my chambermaid.
   She knows that I'm not afraid
   To look at her.
   She is good to me,
   And there's nothing she doesn't see.
   She knows where I'd like to be,
   But it doesn't matter.
   Chorus

4. Now your dancing child with his Chinese suit,
   He spoke to me, I took his flute.
   No, I wasn't very cute to him,
   Was I?
   But I did it, though, because he lied,
   Because he took you for a ride,
   And because time was on his side,
   And because I ...
   Chorus

RAINY DAY WOMEN #12 AND 35

Words & Music by Bob Dylan

stone ya when you're try'n' to go home._____ Then they'll

stone ya when you're there all a - lone._____ But I

would not_____ feel_ so all a - lone,_____

Ev - 'ry - bod - y must get stoned._____ 2. Well, they'll

45

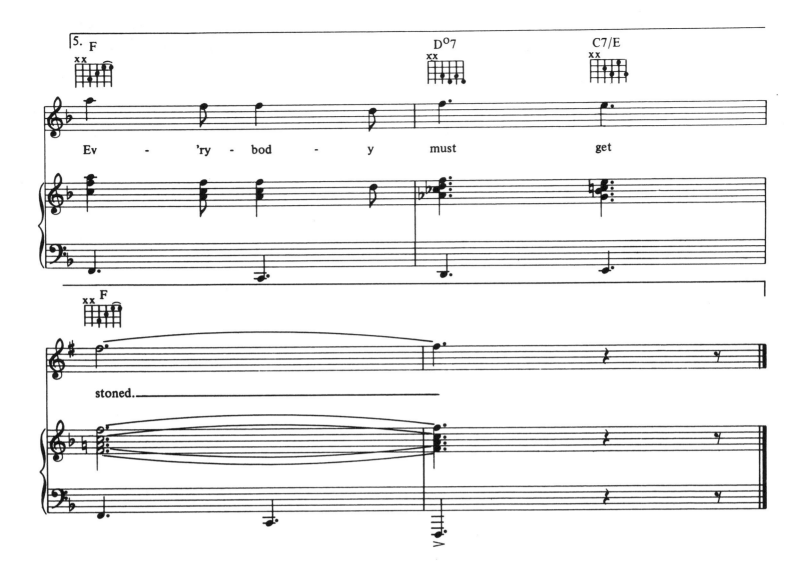

Additional Lyrics

2. Well, they'll stone ya when you're walkin' 'long the street.
   They'll stone ya when you're tryin' to keep your seat.
   They'll stone ya when you're walkin' on the floor.
   They'll stone ya when you're walkin' to the door.
   But I would not feel so all alone,
   Everybody must get stoned.

3. They'll stone ya when you're at the breakfast table.
   They'll stone ya when you are young and able.
   They'll stone ya when you're tryin' to make a buck.
   They'll stone ya and then they'll say, "Good luck."
   Tell ya what, I would not feel so all alone,
   Everybody must get stoned.

4. Well, they'll stone you and say that it's the end.
   Then they'll stone you and then they'll come back again.
   They'll stone you when you're riding in your car.
   They'll stone you when you're playing your guitar.
   Yes, but I would not feel so all alone,
   Everybody must get stoned.

5. Well, they'll stone you when you walk all alone.
   They'll stone you when you are walking home.
   They'll stone you and then say you are brave.
   They'll stone you when you are set down in your grave.
   But I would not feel so all alone,
   Everybody must get stoned.

I'LL BE YOUR BABY TONIGHT

Words & Music by Bob Dylan

night._____ Shut the

Well, that mock-ing-bird's gon-na sail___ a - way,_____

We're gon-na for-get it, That big, fat moon___ is gon - na

shine like a spoon,___ But, we're gon-na let it, You won't re - gret it. Kick your

shoes off,__ Do not fear,__ Bring that bot-

tle o-ver here,__

I'll _____ be your _____ ba-by to -

night. _____

QUINN THE ESKIMO (THE MIGHTY QUINN)

Words & Music by Bob Dylan

Moderately slow, with a steady beat

Verse:

1. Ev-'ry-bod-y's build-ing the big ships and the boats,

Some are build-in' mon - u -ments,_ oth-ers jot-ting down notes.

Ev-'ry-bod-y's in des-pair, ev-'ry girl and boy. But when Quinn, the es-ki-mo gets here, ev-'ry-bod-y's gon-na jump for joy.

Chorus:

Come all with-out, Come all with-in, You'll not see noth-in' like the might-y Quinn.

51

Additional Lyrics

2. I like to do just like the rest,
   I like my sugar sweet,
   But guarding fumes and making haste,
   It ain't my cup of meat.
   Ev'rybody's 'neath the trees feeding pigeons on a limb,
   But when Quinn, the eskimo gets here,
   All the pigeons gonna run to him.
   Chorus

3. A cat's meown, and a cow's moo,
   I can't recite them all.
   Just Tell me where it hurts yuh, honey,
   And I'll tell you who to call.
   Nobody can get no sleep, there's someone on ev'ryone's toes,
   But when the eskimo gets here,
   Ev'rybody's gonna want to doze.
   Chorus

SIMPLE TWIST OF FATE

Words & Music by Bob Dylan

1. They sat to-geth-er in the park, as the eve-ning sky
(Verses 2 & 3 see block lyrics)

grew dark, she looked at him and he felt a spark

tin-gle to his bones. 'Twas then he felt a-lone

and wished that he'd gone straight

and watched out for a sim-ple twist of fate.

Harmonica

4. He woke up, the room was bare, he did-n't see her a-ny-
(Verses 5 & 6 see block lyric)

-where,   he told him-self he did-n't   care,   pushed the win-

-dow o-pen wide,   felt an emp-ti-ness in - - - side,

to which he just could not re-late,

brought on by a sim-ple twist of fate.

1, 2.

Harmonica

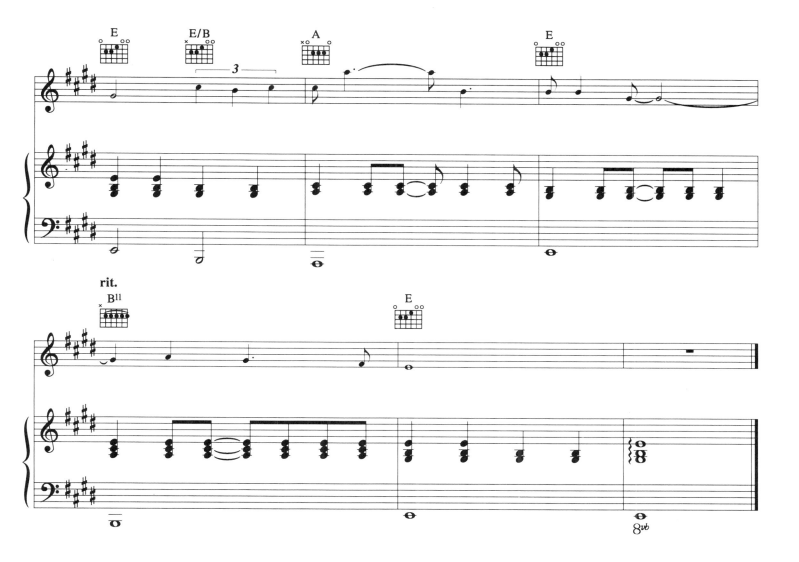

Verse 2:
They walked along by the old canal
A little confused, I remember well
And stopped into a strange hotel with a neon burnin' bright
He felt the heat of the night hit him like a freight train
Moving with a simple twist of fate.

Verse 3:
A saxophone someplace far off played
As she was walkin' on by the arcade
As the light bust through a beat-up shade where he was wakin' up
She dropped a coin into the cup of a blind man at the gate
And forgot about a simple twist of fate.

Verse 5:
He hears the ticking of the clocks
And walks along with a parrot that talks
Hunts her down by the waterfront docks where the sailors all come in
Maybe she'll pick him out again, how long must he wait
One more time for a simple twist of fate.

Verse 6:
People tell me it's a sin
To know and feel too much within
I still believe she was my twin, but I lost the ring
She was born in spring, but I was born too late
Blame it on a simple twist of fate.

HURRICANE

Words by Bob Dylan & Jacques Levy
Music by Bob Dylan

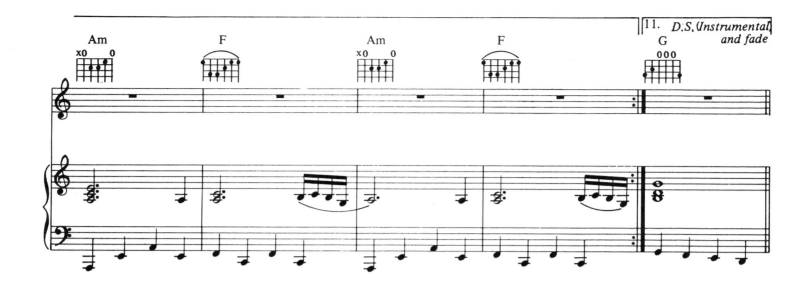

Additional Lyrics

2. Three bodies lyin' there does Patty see,
   And another man named Bello, movin' around mysteriously.
   "I didn't do it," he says, and he throws up his hands,
   "I was only robbin' the register, I hope you understand,
   I saw them leavin'," he says, and he stops.
   "One of us had better call up the cops."
   And so Patty calls the cops,
   And they arrive on the scene with their red lights flashin'
   In the hot New Jersey night.

3. Meanwhile, far away in another part of town,
   Rubin Carter and a couple of friends are drivin' around.
   Number one contender for the middleweight crown,
   Had no idea what kinda shit was about to go down,
   When a cop pulled him over to the side of the road,
   Just like the time before and the time before that.
   In Paterson that's just the way things go,
   If you're black you might as well not show up on the street,
   'Less you wanna draw the heat.

4. Alfred Bello had a partner and he had a rap for the cops,
   Him and Arthur Dexter Bradley were just out prowlin' around.
   He said, "I saw two men runnin' out, they looked like middleweights.
   They jumped into a white car with out-of-state plates."
   And Miss Patty Valentine just nodded her head,
   Cop said, "Wait a minute boys, this one's not dead."
   So they took him to the infirmary,
   And though this man could hardly see,
   They told him that he could identify the guilty men.

5. Four in the mornin' and they haul Rubin in,
   Take him to the hospital and they bring him upstairs.
   The wounded man looks up through his one dyin' eye,
   Says, "Wha'd you bring him in here for? He ain't the guy!"
   Yes, here's the story of the Hurricane,
   The man the authorities came to blame,
   For somethin' that he never done.
   Put in a prison cell, but one time he coulda been
   The champion of the world.

6. **Four months later, the ghettos are in flame,**
   Rubin's in South America, fightin' for his name,
   While Arthur Dexter Bradley's still in the robbery game,
   And the cops are puttin' the screws to him, lookin' for somebody to blame,
   "Remember that murder that happened in a bar?"
   "Remember you said you saw the getaway car?"
   "You think you'd like to play ball with the law?"
   "Think it mighta been that fighter that you saw runnin' that night?"
   "Don't forget that you are white."

7. Arthur Dexter Bradley said, "I'm really not sure,"
   Cops said, "A poor boy like you could use a break.
   We got you for the motel job and we're talkin' to your friend Bello,
   Now you don't wanna have to go back to jail, be a nice fellow.
   You'll be doin' society a favor,
   That sonofabitch is brave and gettin' braver.
   We want to put his ass in stir,
   We want to pin this triple murder on him,
   He ain't no Gentleman Jim."

8. Rubin could take a man out with just one punch,
   But he never did like to talk about it all that much.
   "It's my work," he'd say, "and I do it for pay.
   And when it's over I'd just as soon go on my way,
   Up to some paradise,
   Where the trout streams flow and the air is nice,
   And ride a horse along a trail."
   But then they took him to the jail house,
   Where they try to turn a man into a mouse.

9. All of Rubin's cards were marked in advance,
   The trial was a pig-circus, he never had a chance.
   The judge made Rubin's witnesses drunkards from the slums,
   To the white folks who watched he was a revolutionary bum.
   And to the black folks he was just a crazy nigger,
   No one doubted that he pulled the trigger,
   And though they could not produce the gun,
   The D. A. said he was the one who did the deed.
   And the all-white jury agreed.

10. Rubin Carter was falsely tried,
    The crime was murder-one, guess who testified?
    Bello and Bradley, and they both baldly lied,
    And the newspapers, they all went along for the ride.
    How can the life of such a man
    Be in the palm of some fool's hand?
    To see him obviously framed,
    Couldn't help but make me feel ashamed to live in a land
    Where justice is a game.

11. Now all the criminals in their coats and their ties
    Are free to drink martinis and watch the sun rise,
    While Rubin sits like Buddha in a ten-foot cell,
    An innocent man in a living hell.
    That's the story of the Hurricane,
    But it won't be over till they clear his name,
    And give him back the time he's done,
    Put in a prison cell, but one time he coulda been
    The champion of the world.

CHANGING OF THE GUARDS

Words & Music by Bob Dylan

-fer no re- ward_ when her false i - dols fall (false i-dols fall) and_____

cruel death sur-ren-ders with its pale ghost_ re - treat-

-ing be-tween the King _and the Queen_ of swords.__

Saxophone 2 time only

Fade out

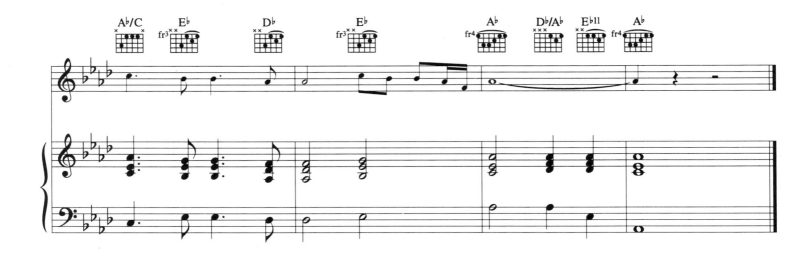

Verse 2:
The cold-blooded moon
The captain waits above the celebration
Sending his thoughts to a beloved maid
Whose ebony face is beyond communication
The captain is down but still believing that his love will be repaid.

They shaved her head
She was torn between Jupiter and Apollo
A messenger arrived with a black nightingale
I seen her on the stairs and I couldn't help but follow
Follow her down past the fountain where they lifted her veil.

Verse 3:
I stumbled to my feet
I rode past destruction in the ditches
With the stitches still mending 'neath a heart-shaped tattoo
Renegade priests and treacherous young witches
Were handing out the flowers that I'd given to you.

The palace of mirrors
Where dog soldiers are reflected
The endless road and the wailing of chimes
The empty rooms where her memory is protected
Where the angels' voices whisper to the souls of previous times.

Verse 4:
She wakes him up
Forty-eight hours later, the sun is breaking
Near broken chains, mountain laurel and rolling rocks
She's begging to know what measures he now will be taking
He's pulling her down and she's clutching on to his long golden locks.

Gentlemen, he said
I don't need your organization, I've shined your shoes
I've moved your mountains and marked your cards
But Eden is burning, either get ready for elimination
Or else your hearts must have the courage for the changing of the guards.

LICENSE TO KILL

Words & Music by Bob Dylan

1. Man thinks cos he rules the earth— he can
(Verses 2 & 3 see block lyrics)

do with it as he please—— and if things don't— change soon,

he will.— Oh,— man has in-vent-ed his doom,— first

step was touch-ing the moon.— Now there's a wo-man on my block, she just sit

there as the night grows still, she say who___ gon-na take a-way his li-cense to

1, 2.

kill?___ 2. Now they kill.___ May-be

3.

noise-mak-er, spir-it-mak-er, heart-break-er, back-break-er, leave no stone un-turned,_ may-be an

ac-tor in a plot that might be all that you got 'til your er-ror you clear-ly learned.—

4. Now he wor-ships at an al - tar

of a stag - nant pool and when he sees his re-flec-tion, he's ful -

- filled. Oh, man is op-posed to fair play,—— he wants it

all and he wants it his way.— Now there's a wo-man— on my block she just sit

there as the night grows still.— She say who— gon-na take a-way his li-cense to

kill?—

Harmonica

Verse 2:

Now, they take him and they teach him and they groom him for life
And they set him on a path where he's bound to get ill
Then they bury him with stars
Sell his body like they do used cars.

Now, there's a woman on my block
She just sit there facin' the hill
She say who gonna take away his license to kill?

Verse 3:

Now, he's hell-bent for destruction, he's afraid and confused
And his brain has been mismanaged with great skill
All he believes are his eyes
And his eyes, they just tell him lies.

But there's a woman on my block
Sittin' there in a cold chill
She say who gonna take away his license to kill?

SILVIO

Words & Music by Bob Dylan & Robert Hunter

snap my fin-gers and re-quire the rain_ From a clear blue sky and turn it
tell you fan-cy, I can tell you plain,_ You give some-thing up for ev-'ry-

off a-gain._ I can stroke your bo-dy and re-lieve your pain,_
thing you gain._ Since ev-'ry plea-sure's got an edge of pain,_

Charm the_ whis-tle off an eve-ning train._
Pay for your tick-et and don't com-plain._ Sil - vi - o,

sil - ver and gold_ won't buy back the beat of a heart_ grown cold._

Coda

dead men know._ Sil - vi - o, sil - ver and gold_ won't

buy back the beat of a heart___ grown cold.___

Sil - vi - o, I got - ta go___

find out some - thing on - ly dead men know.___

repeat and fade

81

DIGNITY

Words & Music by Bob Dylan

1. Fat man look-in' in a_____ blade
(Verse 2 see block lyric)

of steel, thin man look-in' at his last meal,

hol - low man look-in' in a cot - ton - field___ for

dig - ni - ty.___

Bridge 1. Some-bo - dy got mur-dered on___ New Year's Eve,

some-bo - dy said dig-ni - ty was the first to leave,

83

I went in-to the ci-ty, went into the town, went into the

land of the mid-night— sun.

3. Search - in' high,— search - in' low,—

search - in' ev-ery - where— I know,

ask-in' the cops_ wher - ev-er I go,_ have you_____ seen dig-

-ni-ty?

4. Blind man break-in'   out of a trance,   puts both his hands in the pock-ets
(Verses 5, 7 & 8 see block lyrics)

of chance,   hop-in' to find one cir-cum-stance_   of

wasn't a-ny dif-ference to___ me.___

6. Chil-ly wind sharp as a raz - or blade,   house on fire,___

debts un - paid,___   gon-na stand at the win-dow,   gon-na ask the maid,

have you   seen dig - ni - ty?___

bor - der towns___ of des - pair.___

9. Got no place to fade, got no coat,—

I'm on the rol - lin' riv - er in a jerk - in' boat,—

tryin' to read a note   some-bo-dy wrote   'bout dig - ni - ty. __

10. Sick man look-in' for the doc - tor's cure,
(Verse 11 see block lyric)

look-in' at his hands —— for the lines that —— were, ——

and in-to ev-'ry mas-ter-piece of lit-er-a-ture for

dig - ni - ty. ——

1.

2.

Bridge 4. Some-one showed me a pic - ture and I just laughed,—

dig - ni - ty nev - er been pho - to - graphed, I

went in - to the red, went in - to the black, in-to the

val-ley of — dry bone dreams.—

91

12. So ma-ny roads,— so much at stake, so ma-ny dead ends, I'm at

the edge of the lake, some-times I won-der—

what it's gon-na take to find— dig-ni - ty.—

Repeat to fade

Verse 2:
Wise man lookin' in a blade of grass
Young man lookin' in the shadows that pass
Poor man lookin' through painted glass
For dignity.

Verse 5:
I went to the wedding of Mary-Lou
She said "I don't want nobody see me talkin' to you"
Said she could get killed if she told me what she knew
About dignity.

Verse 7:
Drinkin' man listens to the voice he hears
In a crowded room full of covered up mirrors
Lookin' into the lost forgotten years
For dignity.

Verse 8:
Met Prince Phillip at the home of the blues
Said he'd give me information if his name wasn't used
He wanted money up front, said he was abused
By dignity.

Bridge 3:
Footprints runnin' cross the silver sand
Steps goin' down into tattoo land
I met the sons of darkness and the sons of light
In the bordertowns of despair.

Verse 11:
Englishman stranded in the blackheart wind
Combin' his hair back, his future looks thin
Bites the bullet and he looks within
For dignity.

NOT DARK YET

Words & Music by Bob Dylan

Moderately slow, with a beat

1. Shad - ows are fall - ing and I've been here all day

2. - 5. *See additional lyrics*

It's too hot to sleep__ time is run - ning a - way__

It's not dark yet,—— but it's—— get-ting there

but it's—— get-ting there

rit.

Additional lyrics

2. Well my sense of humanity has gone down the drain
Behind every beautiful thing there's been some kind of pain
She wrote me a letter and she wrote it so kind
She put down in writing what was in her mind
I just don't see why I should even care
It's not dark yet, but it's getting there

3. Well, I've been to London and I've been to gay Paree
I've followed the river and I got to the sea
I've been down on the bottom of a world full of lies
I ain't looking for nothing in anyone's eyes
Sometimes my burden seems more than I can bear
It's not dark yet, but it's getting there

4. *Instrumental solo*

5. I was born here and I'll die here against my will
I know it looks like I'm moving, but I'm standing still
Every nerve in my body is so vacant and numb
I can't even remember what it was I came here to get away from
Don't even hear a murmur of a prayer
It's not dark yet, but it's getting there.